J. PATRICK LEWIS & GARY KELLEY

Creative Editions

In **SEPTEMBER**, three hundred gangly innocents shipped out by Channel steamer from Southampton to Boulogne. Then, wedged in by heat, sweat, and stink, we rode for hours by cattle car at cattle speed, wheels click-clacking across France.

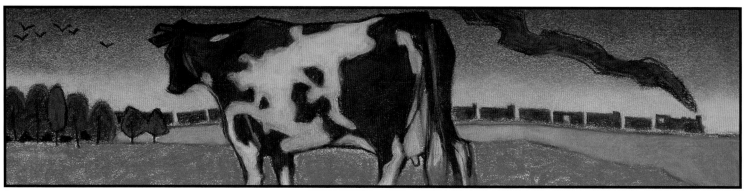

The **TRAIN** hissed to a stop, and its slat-ted doors flew open. We marched ten miles through Belgium to the Western Front—a planet away from Cardiff, Wales, and the meadows of my youth.

1914 would be a bad year for dreaming.

CARDIFF 400 km

By **OCTOBER**, we had descended into our new home, five hundred miles of trenches tunneling terror.

In **NOVEMBER**, grief arrived on the second hand, by sniper, shell, sleet, and snow.

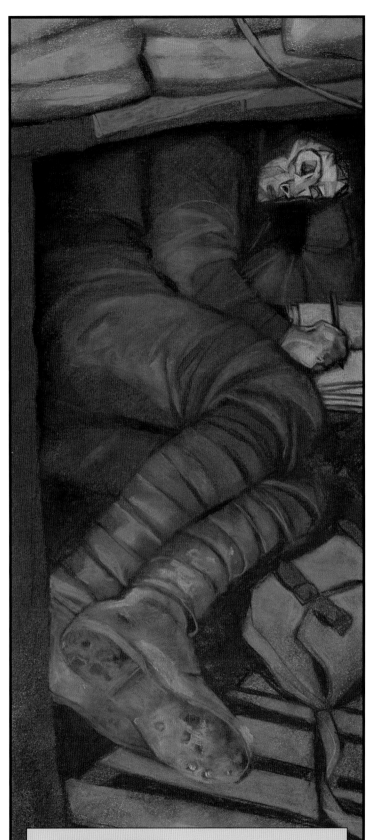

In **DECEMBER**, lying doggo each morning in my serpentine cellar, I wrote in the gilded daybook that had been my father's parting gift. Staring at my iced-over daisies, I wondered if my German mate across no man's land nursed trench foot too.

Like **PHANTOMS** dimly spied through the shroud fog, the surrounding villages, dark in daylight, became eerie husks under an unforgiving moon. They had been bombed, battered, and emptied of humanity.

MORNINGS, trench rats fattened on corpses or live ears. Nights, lice bit into our subterranean dreams.

NOISE like a hurricane turned us inside out. Machine-gun fire, the whizz-bang of the field guns, reconnaissance planes droning overhead, orders screamed up and down the line. The constant clamor made *silence* seem a quaint word.

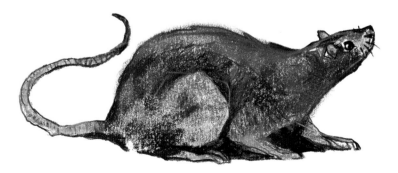

The **FROZEN** ground above became a bone orchard for soldiers running on raids —and falling like ninepins quick with lead.

As **CHRISTMAS** approached, Princess Mary surprised nearly half a million British boys with brass boxed treasures of writing materials, tobacco, and chocolate. From Mother came a tin of Cardiff's finest rhubarb cheese crumble and a scribbled note.

Dear darlin' Owen,
You'll be getting a crumble
twice a month, son, if you
promise to sit yourself
down here with the
Davies clan and sing for
us all next Christmas.
Yr bleedin' Ma

I HAD a fair voice, some said. One that might well win favor with the London Choral Society. Yet this war welcomed no melody.

CHRISTMAS Eve morning stumbled out of dark's rougher neighborhoods. The sunlight that dazzled our corner of the cold did little to brighten another afternoon of despair.

By **DUSK**, the artillery had fallen strangely silent. One of our fusiliers peeked above the rampart. Over the humps of the dead and wounded, he spotted small, candlelit pines ghosting the German line.

BEFORE we could fathom the meaning of the trees, friendly insults flew our way. Soon, daft retorts from both sides mellowed into actual greetings.

Happy Christmas to you!

Come over here, Englishmen.

No, you come over.

Then the **FROSTED AIR** crackled with the sound of a German baritone singing *Stille Nacht—Silent Night*. My tripwire heart plinked like a piano string. We stood stunned in the electric night.

I LISTENED, mustered my mettle, and returned a tenor *First Noel*. Friend and foe clapped at my performance, as if serenading an enemy was the most natural thing.

A **BRAVE** unarmed German climbed from his dugout and began a slow march over forbidden ground. A member of the Scots Guards did the same.

So **EMBOLDENED**, dozens and then hundreds of us took our first halting steps toward a court-martial offense on both sides: fraternizing with the enemy.

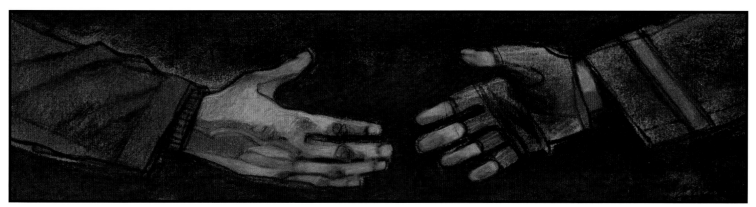

I CRAWLED up and shuffled toward my first Hun. We stared at each other, two baffled amateurs playing at professional slaughter.

THEN, the strangest thing: With a shaking hand, he offered me a most inviting gift—a chocolate bar. I admired the buttons on his tunic, and he mine. Without a word, we both clipped off two of them and made fair exchange.

HE slipped a browned photograph from his wallet.

A **SOLDIER** somersaulted over the German parapet—a clown in the land of the lost. He tumbled and spun over now common ground and pulled from his belt four tent stakes which he juggled flawlessly, drawing cheers.

The **CIRCUS** performer swashbuckled a bow and returned to the trench.

Bravo!

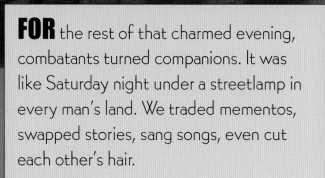

FOR the rest of that charmed evening, combatants turned companions. It was like Saturday night under a streetlamp in every man's land. We traded mementos, swapped stories, sang songs, even cut each other's hair.

NO ONE wanted it to end.

DAWN broke cold. The Germans pitched in to chip the iced earth for our lads' graves. We did likewise for theirs.

AFTER that grisly business came some morning cheer. Two soldiers struggled up, hefting one of the abandoned sows that often rooted through outlying towns.

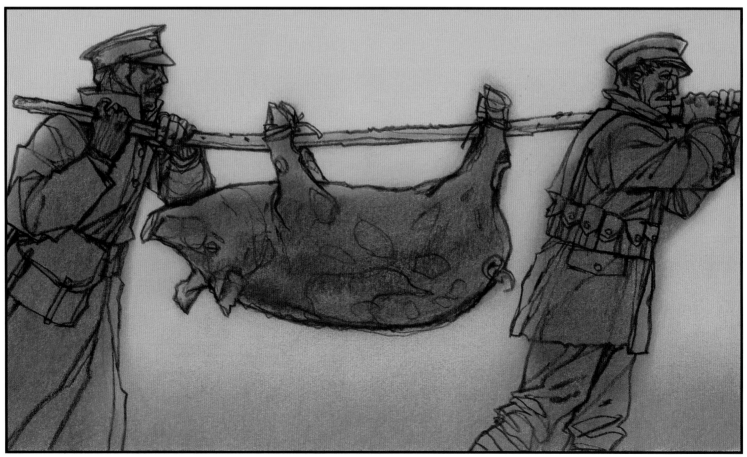

A makeshift **SPIT** appeared. We met in the middle of the hushed moonscape—Jerries and Tommies alike—to share Christmas Day dinner of unlucky pig and Maconochie stew. Strange warriors, briefly at peace, tucked into hock and ham like Roman emperors.

A **FOOTBALL** game broke out. But peals of laughter announced our "treason," arousing the brass hats to fury.

FIELD OFFICERS mostly saw the truce as tomfoolery. Still, our major, till then pretending not to notice, had had enough and bellowed us back to the rat tunnels.

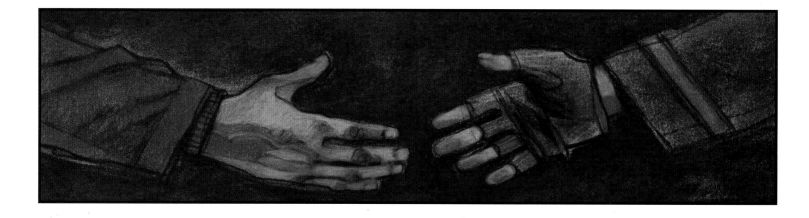

WE turned away—backward glances from both sides—and watched our flourishing fellowship, the tag end of war-weary hope, perish like a pinched candle flame.

On **BOXING DAY**, December 26, some sectors extended the truce. Not ours.

Our **CAPTAIN** stood on the parapet, fired three shots in the air, and held up a banner.

His **GERMAN** counterpart, raising an answering standard, fired two shots.

And **THE WAR** resumed. No man's land once again became the moonlit desert of the dead.

A **HARD-NOSED PRUSSIAN** unit, ignorant of the pause, callous to the cause, had settled in behind its barbed wire. Standing on the firing step to take over the watch, I was daydreaming about how spring in Wales would be welcoming me back before the moorlands greened. About how noble it would be if the truce stopped the fighting for good. The powers of circumstance then called my name.

A **SNIPER'S BULLET** flew the killing ground and shattered the top of my spine, carrying me from the earth on that voyage all creatures must take.

The **REGIMENT** chaplain knelt down beside me in the duckboard mud. He mumbled a short prayer "for Owen Davies, the Christmas truce singer." Then he pulled the daybook from the side pocket of my tunic, intent on sending it back to Wales. It fell open to the last entry.

MORE than 30 countries sent soldiers to the European battlefields of World War I (1914–1918). Nearly 10 million soldiers were killed on those battlefields by bullet, shell, bayonet, gas, or illness. Some of the bloodiest and most unrelenting combat occurred along the Western Front—a battle line that snaked hundreds of miles across Belgium and France. West of this line were the Allies—mostly British and French soldiers. East of the line were Germans and Austro-Hungarians. Each side dug out vast networks of trenches in which troops could move around and avoid enemy fire. Between the two sides was a narrow, empty corridor—a killing field called "no man's land." As the enemies became entrenched, neither could gain territory, and the Western Front remained virtually unchanged throughout the war. On Christmas Eve 1914, the war briefly ended at numerous points along the Front when enemies put down their rifles and gas masks and came together in fellowship. The Christmas truce occurred 6 months into the war; the killing continued for 47 months afterwards. This story features a fictional narrator and takes place near Ypres, Belgium.

Text copyright © 2011 J. Patrick Lewis   Illustrations copyright © 2011 Gary Kelley

Published in 2011 by Creative Editions   P.O. Box 227, Mankato, MN 56002 USA

Creative Editions is an imprint of The Creative Company.

Designed by Rita Marshall with Gary Kelley   Edited by Aaron Frisch

Library of Congress Cataloging-in-Publication Data

Lewis, J. Patrick.   And the soldiers sang / by J. Patrick Lewis; illustrations by Gary Kelley.

Summary: A young Welsh soldier fights along the Western Front during World War I, experiencing the horrors of trench warfare before participating in the famed Christmas Truce of 1914.   ISBN 978-1-56846-220-2

1. World War, 1914-1918—Campaigns—Western Front—Juvenile fiction. 2. Christmas Truce, 1914—Juvenile fiction. [1. World War, 1914-1918—Campaigns—Western Front—Fiction. 2. Christmas Truce, 1914—Fiction.]

I. Kelley, Gary, ill. II. Title.

PZ7.L5866An 2011   [Fic]—dc22   2010028644   CPSIA: 120110 PO1405

First edition   9 8 7 6 5 4 3 2 1

Christmas Eve, 1914

I am twenty years old today and witnessed a miracle. Will anyone believe that tonight I sang a carol to the German Army and to great applause? Tomorrow is Christmas! It looks like I'll be heading home very soon.

THE chaplain closed the diary and stuck it in his coat. He shut my eyes and hurried down the line.

CHAPLAINS were busy men in the Great War.